Fred's TV

Written and Illustrated by Clive Dobson

ISBN 0-920668-59-3 (Soft cover)
ISBN 0-920668-60-7 (Hard cover)

FIREFLY BOOKS

A Firefly Book

Published by
Firefly Books Ltd.
250 Sparks Avenue
Willowdale, Ontario, Canada
M2H 2S4

Design: DUO Strategy and Design Inc.
Printed and bound in Canada

This book is dedicated
to all species...
birds and humans.

Fred sat down in front of the television with enough supplies to last the whole weekend. He had a can of bright-colored pop, six black cookies oozing white cream, a package of purple foaming pellets, and a huge, lumpy ball of gum.

Sometimes his school friends kept him company in front of the glowing tube. They didn't say much and they didn't play much. They just sat there, stupefied.

One day, Fred's parents said that this was too much. They decided that he could only watch television for one hour each day. . . no more! But when his parents were busy, he went back to watching TV anyway, hour after hour, program after program.

Fred's father got angry.

He unplugged the television and carried it down to the storage room in the basement.

Several days later, when Fred was missing at dinnertime, his parents found him curled up between some cardboard boxes, watching TV.

Fred's Dad was furious. He couldn't think of anything else to do, except to drag the television outside to the back yard. It wasn't a very good idea.

It rained that night.

Fred came downstairs in the morning to watch TV. Then he remembered where it was. Out the back door he ran, extension cord in hand.

He plugged in the television and flicked on the switch. BANG! Smelly white smoke billowed from the back of the set. There was no picture, so Fred turned the TV off.

For the next week or so, Fred was never at home. He stayed at his friend's house watching TV until he wasn't welcome anymore. Fred begged and pleaded with his Mom and Dad to have their TV fixed.

So, a TV repairman came by. He was surprised to see the TV in the back yard. He told Fred that it would be expensive to fix, and he took the insides back to the repair shop.

Fred sat there eating his toast, staring sadly at the empty cabinet. Before he finished, a skinny blackbird landed on top of the TV and watched him cautiously.

The bird flew away when Fred offered it something to eat. "I'll put these crusts inside the TV where they won't get wet," thought Fred. "Just in case he comes back. He looks very hungry."

The blackbird did come back when Fred was at school. If there hadn't been a light snow that day, Fred might not have noticed the little footprints on top of the TV. He was quite amazed.

He looked inside. The bread crusts were gone.

"Maybe he'll come back again," thought Fred. He ran into the kitchen to get more bread. After waiting patiently for half an hour, he began to get cold and went inside the house for his own dinner.

Before he went to sleep, he looked out of his bedroom window one last time to see if his hungry friend had returned.

Snow was falling again and the television looked strange outside in the back yard. The bread was still where he had left it.

As Fred drifted off to sleep, he wondered how all of the other birds in the city were going to find anything to eat with deep snow covering the ground.

Winter light of morning came slowly. The deep snow outside muffled the usual traffic noises. Different sounds from the back yard brought Fred to the window. There were two blackbirds on top of the TV and three inside. They had eaten all of the bread and were calling out for more.

Fred ran down to the kitchen, grabbed a loaf of bread and rushed out the back door into the snow. The blackbirds were startled by the sudden movement and flew up to the telephone wires.

The snow slipped down his boots and froze his bare ankles. Quickly he tore up some bread and dashed back inside to watch. All five blackbirds came back, and with them two sparrows and a pigeon.

Fred watched them until his Dad came downstairs to make breakfast. From a shelf, he pulled down a bottle of cornmeal and handed it to Fred. Then he smiled and pointed toward the back door.

By mid-winter, there were many different kinds of birds coming by regularly for food. Even a pair of cardinals visited Fred's TV feeder once a day on their rounds.

Every morning the chickadees wake Fred up for sunflower seeds.

Fred's Dad doesn't yell at him anymore. He even bought a new color television for everyone in the family. Sometimes he teases Fred and asks with a smile on his face, ''You still watching that old TV?''

Once in a while Fred does watch the new television, but only when the old TV in the back yard has gone off the air for the evening.

About Clive Dobson
Clive was born in 1949 in Winnipeg, Manitoba. He grew up in the country, but now lives in Toronto with his wife and two children. Clive creates freelance illustrations for newspapers and magazines, has had a one-man show of his paintings at the Hamilton, Ontario, Art Gallery, and is the author of *Feeding Wild Birds in Winter*.